K. C. Wilson

Songs of Many Days

K. C. Wilson

Songs of Many Days

ISBN/EAN: 9783744768863

Printed in Europe, USA, Canada, Australia, Japan

Cover: Foto ©Andreas Hilbeck / pixelio.de

More available books at **www.hansebooks.com**

SONGS OF MANY DAYS

SONGS OF MANY DAYS

By K. C.

" Look then into thine heart and write."—LONGFELLOW.

𝔏𝔬𝔫𝔡𝔬𝔫:

MARCUS WARD & CO., 67, 68, CHANDOS STREET

AND ROYAL ULSTER WORKS, BELFAST

1882

To the Memory of

MY MOTHER,

WITH EVERLASTING LOVE AND REVERENCE.

"Sad all, and soft in the moonlight of Memory, the lost Loved One all in the right, as we now see, we all in the wrong.

"The departed are still with us; are not both they and we in the hand of God? A little while and we shall all meet."

T. CARLYLE.

CONTENTS.

8   CONTENTS.

THE DAUGHTERS OF PRŒTUS.

ARGUMENT.

The three daughters of Prœtus, King of Argos, were stricken with
madness by Dionysus in consequence of their despising his worship.
The King applied to Melampus for assistance in their recovery,
which was effected by pursuing them, with shouting and singing,
from Argos to Mount Sicyon.

"OH! struggle! sweet as to the mountaineer
The breasting of a skyward-towered height,
Where wild, familiar winds come rushing down,
Like foes to turn him from their fastnesses,
And still he presses upward, upward still,
Divining the victorious end of toil,
The high, deep silences against the blue!"
   Thus I, Melampus, sang as on we sped
Toward the mountain-goal of Sicyon;
And, still pursuing, still more clearly sang,
   "'Tis victory that shall requite our toil!
Know this, ye men of Argolis, ye sons
Of heroes who at Colchis did the deed;
Whose god-like hearts sprang upward to the skies,
When o'er the sea the lyre's wild music swept

B

Their pæans of fearless greeting to the foe!
Sing now, as victors sing! the end is good!
E'en now they faintlier run, they droop, they lag!
Iphianassa there! behold, she lags!
Lysippe wearies, wearies of the way,
And sweet Iphinoë for ever droops;
Ye gods, because upon my heart I bear
The woe of divination, I foreknow
Amid what fadeless flowers she shall rest
For ever from the anguish of this day!
Content thee, King, for thou hast seen thy last
Of her sweet eyes: three daughters fled from thee,
And two come home once more the morrow-morn;
And lo, the end is good!"   Yea, thus I sang,
And all about me cried, "The end is good!"
And still pursuing, once again I sang,
      "Is not the scorn revenged? now stay thy hand;
Thine, Dionysus, is their reverence,
And the first sacrifice unto thy name
The blood of this land's helpless infancy!
But for the end, what woe, what woe were ours!"
      And all about me cried, "The end is good!"
And hasted evermore; and evermore
The women fled before our flying feet
O'er mead and rock, o'er stream and tangled bank,
Past leafy refuges of frighted birds,
Past fragrant haunts of nodding flow'rs, still on,
And knew not any beauty of the earth

For the wild madness of their darkened souls.
And as with song and shout we hasted by,
Behold! they lagged, and fell, and rose again,
And, staggering toward the goal, perceived
Within their souls the glimmer of a light
That flooded all the present pain with shame;
Then, at the foot of Sicyon, turned round
To front us with their faint, exhausted looks,
And lo! within their tirèd eyes we saw
Reason again, and knew the deed was done!
And the just gods took sweet Iphinoë.
   Then once again I sang, "Behold her dead!
O blest is she who hath attained her rest;
Who 'mid the hills and dales Elysian
Wand'reth, and knoweth not of night or day,
Or chilly barrenness of nature's want,
Desire unfulfilled or joy delayed;
Who hath received the All of Hope and Love,
And 'mid a fadeless glory of content
Divines the Presence of Supremest Rest.
   Ah! blest is she; belovèd of the gods!"
   And they about me cried, "Just are the gods!"
And once again I sang, "The end is good!
Though some may weep, and some may yearn for death
To end this agony of weariness,
And some may recollect their motherhood,
And know the empty home, the murdered ones
Whose faintest cry was a belovèd sound;

And some may lay them down with breaking hearts,
And wish the end had been no less than death!
But the great gods are just! Unto the true
From out life's failures springs a wider trust!
Lo! sorrows are just blessings of the gods,
Divinely sent, lest we forget and fail,
And miss the full reward of perfect rest
Death gives unto endurance to the end!"
    And all with tears cried out, "The gods are just!"
And laid them down, and rested, and rose up,
And passed again in silence to their homes!

ANTIGONE.

ARGUMENT.

When Œdipus, in despair at the fate that had driven him to murder
his father and marry his mother, had put out his eyes and been
expelled from Thebes, he was guided to Attica by his daughter,
Antigone. After her father's death Antigone returned to Thebes,
where she found that her two brothers, Polynices and Eteocles,
had killed each other in single combat while struggling for the
vacant throne. Their interment having been forbidden by Creon,
the succeeding king, Antigone alone ventured to defy the impious
command, and buried the body of Polynices. She was in consequence condemned to be shut up in a cave, whereupon she killed
herself. Her lover, Hæmon, son of Creon, hearing of her death,
slew himself at her side.

O MELANCHOLY life of fated woe!
O miserable death! How like a bird,
That, prisoned from the skies, against the bars
Beats its soft wings and cares not for the hurt,
Could I against these dark, unlovely walls
Despoil myself of tender womanhood!
But faint am I with all this weight of woe,
Too faint to strive, to struggle against Death!
Too faint for aught save here to sit and wait—
A weak, wan misery—approaching doom!

And yet I am not utterly unblest,
In that no sin hath earned such suffering.
Hapless are they who hold not in their hearts
A higher law than e'er divined by man;
And though the words were uttered by the King,
A knowledge kinglier far from me constrained
That pitiful last service unto Death.
And he is buried now! Yea, for the bond
Of brotherhood and home between our lives,
The far-off, childish days, I did the deed
That gave him gentle burial at the last!
Ah! how are these knees worn! how these thin hands!
All night, unweariedly, I toiling knelt
Until no more the terrible, dead Thing
Was seen; no more that ashen, loveless face,
Whereon so deep the sculptor-hand of death
Had graven its hard lines of bitter hate.
Then lo! the end; for they, who at their posts
So long contentedly had slept, awoke,
And seized me thence to bring me here to die!
O miserable Death! And I so young,
So unaccustomed to those things of life
That young hearts love to waken to, and feel
The trembling eyelids of their being uplift
To front the shining gaze of happiness.
So young! so young! and oh! so far away
From those to whom the end of days might be
An end acceptable! through weariness

Of disappointments, and the things of life
That dull the first, ideal colouring;
Those silent griefs that crown the royal brows
Of beautiful Endurance; the wan pain
That moves the fretted soul to long for death,
For Hades! and its sombre quietudes;
And unattainable, disturbless heights
Whence gods look down upon the striving throng!
But I am young; I could have loved my life,
And even now, so near its bitter end,
Take comfort to myself in blessèd dreams
Of all the faint and scanty tastes of joy
Rounded to days of perfect loveliness.
Now joy no more for me! Now nevermore
Those first, sweet lights that shone upon my heart,
The sun-glow; and the happy eyes of eve
That watched me thread the tender olive groves;
The warm, clear waters lapping 'gainst my throat,
As, trembling at mine own eyes on myself,
I slipped my shining raiment and slid down
Amid the naiads within the secret pool;
To hear no more bird-melodies of joy,
That, as the day wore into dewy eve,
To silence sank, as notes from Orpheus' lyre
Still ever faintlier breathed across the sea
Her heroes' last farewell to Argolis!
Now nevermore to meet the eyes of love!
Alas! ye gods, this hunger of my heart,

Beyond all craving of these hapless lips
For bread and water to once more renew
My famished strength; this yearning, over-brimmed
With hopelessness of hope; and longing love
Sick with mute sadness and the certainty
Of endless separation. I loved him!
That god-like Hæmon ! Though the curse was mine,
And wedded days of measureless content
Might never merge my soul within his soul;
And the soft touches of his children's hands
Could never crown my years with motherhood,
I loved him! At the first, divining not
Fate's dark Erinnyes over-shading all,
Love gave to us his priceless gifts of love;
Unquestioning surrender unto joy,
Communings, and the tender nearnesses
Of hand to hand and trembling lip to lip;
Yet as I clearer apprehended Fate,
Apart I passed, and held my life aloof,
Lest it should draw his too beneath the curse.
But with the outward breaking of a bond
Love does not always cease; nor is it dead
Because still silences possess its place;
Nay; rather like the flower thro' winter days,
In darkling quiet it renews itself
Beyond all former beauty, till the time
When, to perfection come, it pierces earth
And sees the high, illimitable blue.

So love the fuller filled my aching days,
And when the king, his father, bade us part,
Diverse and mute we went, and, stranger-like,
Passed by ungreeting ; while, unstranger-like,
The stolen glances, sweeter for being stol'n,
Traversed the unseen paths 'tween heart and heart
And thrilled the inmost centre of my being.
But far apart and seldom came to us
Such landmarks o'er the weary stretch of days,
And now no more! I know he joyed in them,
And will be sad to miss my little life
And tremulous endeavour of these eyes
To breathe the passion of their love to him.
Ah! deepest pang to me of death and woe !
No more to labour in his life's behalf!
For what is Love, and all of Life to Love,
Unless to it be giv'n to minister
In services of love? to know some part—
Most blest the larger part—itself hath spent
In faithful deeds towards some other life ?
Hath set alight its own self-sacrifice,
And seen the soul rise nearer to the gods
For that perception of the link that holds
All, everywhere, within its wide, warm reach ?
I know he will be sad, and yet no more
Can I prevail in ministry to him ;
For all the tender, passing things that make
The sum of life's sweet service, end in death—

And I so faint, so desolate am left,
That to myself I seem no more than Death
Lost in mortality and seeking home !
O refuge ! o'er the restlessness I yearn,
And, child-like, wearied out with little life,
Lie down and sob myself to dreamless sleep !

THAMYRIS.

ARGUMENT.

A bard of Thrace, who, presuming to surpass the Muses in song, was
deprived of his sight and the power of singing.

O BROKEN-HEARTED one! No more to spend
The thought in song as free as that of birds
That fill the flower-months with melody.
Blind as Tiresias! than him more sad!
Having no golden staff to lead me right,
No favour from the gods to soothe this ache!
How could a mortal think to breathe a strain
Divinely musical as that which touched
The heart of Heav'n and earth; for which the sea,
The rivers hushed themselves? Ah! hapless thought!
How could a mortal strive to reach such heights,
Nor suffer for the deed? Lo! sorrow fell
On those, ere me, who fronted the vain wish:
Fate, inexorable as now, from every brow
Took off its royal crown of womanhood,
And voiceless left each heart to bear its woe
Of alien, unknown naturity.

This I forgot; and how, whilst every maid
Against the voices of the Sacred Nine
Lifted fain notes, great Theia veiled her eyes,
And darkness palpable fell over earth.
This I forgot! And all the afterwoe
Of punishment; the painful suffering,
The loss of tenderer humanity,
The mournful ways, and weary stretch of wings
Unto those marshy wastes where clanging cranes
'Mid desolation lived! This I forgot,
Or deemed my gift above all other gifts
From hands immortal unto mortals giv'n;
A joy imperishable, Love and Light,
More pure, more high, more full of wide content,
And natural outpouring of all thought
Than those clear notes whose careless triumph shook
The listening silences of Helicon;
For as I sang, it seemed that I perceived
The flowers of Olympus in the path,
Their deathless dewdrops lave my mortal feet,
To strengthen them unto still freer heights;
The gods, approving, round me listening leant,
And I, sublime in thus achieving good,
Feared not to face their mute sublimity!
So, rapt in unrealities, I sang;
With face uplifted, as a summer bird
Touched by some topmost joy of joy; glad eyes
Half-wet with too deep tenderness of thought;

Lips tremulous, whence music, unaware
Of all save rapture of expression, sprang
To speech unlimited; and as I sang,
Earth I forgot, and Fame, desirèd once,
And listening Deities; all falsenesses,
All little aims, all weaker purposes;
And, only knowing that my human heart
Held something more than human, poured it forth
In that untaught simplicity that breathes
Most perfect feeling! Happiness was mine!
When lo! but scarce aware of such content,
A sudden blackness fell upon my soul,
And struck me ever into songless grief,
And sightless melancholy of despair!
Dumb! blind! alas! woe, woe; dumb! blind! I stood
And groped for thought, until, with dull, slow sense,
I heard the by-ward trailing of soft robes,
The rhythmic treading of immortal feet
Come near, pass on, and die away from sound,
Till silence and the vasty solitude
With a great horror whelmed me, for behold!
The Sacred Nine had left me to my woe!
O hapless lot! They suffer who would climb
Beyond the heights apportioned to calm life;
Those sovran heights given to few to reach,
Where bitter-sweet of isolation broods,
Companionèd for ever, yet alone!
They suffer who forego contented Thought

To strive, and if to fail, ah! yet to strive,
Though with the anguish of a yearning soul
That sees, and knows, and feels the higher joy,
Far-off, far-off, and scarce to be attained.
Oh! solitary times of foiled delight!
Yet sweeter those—with the rewarded hours
Of fancies, lovely as Acanthus flow'rs,
And voices, breathing music so divine,
So sweet, that, o'er the touch of earth, the soul
Hangs tremulous, as perfect tears of joy
Upon the perfect eyelids of a god—
Than the unquestioning content of thought
That struggles not to reach the awful stars!
Beyond my lot of happiness I yearned
And fell to woe. Unutterable pain!
In even-tones of common speech this voice
Drones on; and still within my soul I feel
Song throb! How animate, how strong, how sweet!
With yearning melody o'er these heart-strings
It wells; and, sea-like 'gainst earth's rocky front,
Entreating sobs and will not be denied.
Alas! dumb heart that may not ever sing,
Dumb soul that may not ever see again!
How are the portals to contentment closed,
And I abandoned by the saving gods,
And broken-hearted as the lyre that fell
In shattered beauty from my nerveless hand!

THE LAST RIDE OF JUANINA.

Forth rode Juanina !
And her gallant horse's feet,
With their steady, rhythmic beat,
    Was the only sound that stirred
Through the brooding summer heat.

Not a bird found heart to sing,
Not a leaf, on lightest wing,
    E'er so timidly disturbed
Nature's breathless slumbering.

Forth rode Juanina !
Down into the forest deep,
To the very soul of sleep,
    Till a thrill of pity stirred
    Heart of leaflet, flower, and bird,
And the winds arose to pray
Such a fair, young life away,
        " Juanina, ~
        Haste away !"

Still with rising fear to pray,
    "Gallop, Juanina!
Gallop for your life away!"

        Hold him, Juanina!
Was it Hell that seemed to roar,
Behind, beside, above, before!
    Flashing forks of blazing fire,
    Winds that circled higher, higher;
Storm-drops beating, like hard hands
Importunate in their demands!
        Hold him, Juanina!
His bloodshot eyes with horror start,
Fear's madnesses seize on his heart.
His ears lie straight against his neck,
Foam-splashes hither, thicker fleck
The straining cords of leg and chest!
            Juanina,
Downward lean upon your breast,
Lower, lower, lower yet!
There is many a groaning bough
Fain to touch your soft, white brow.
        Juanina, lower yet!
And you can not? Hold your breath,
One prayer, one sigh, and this is Death,
            Juanina!

Ah ! earth is so still again !
   Only here and there some leaf,
   With soft petulance of grief,
Shakes its silver fringe of rain ;
And a low wind 'mid the trees
Sobs its saddest melodies ;
And a song-bird down the wood,
   Flying, flying, flying,
Lights and sings in raptured mood
   Its ineffable delight ;
Lights, and sings, and troubles not
Lest it wake you from your sleep,
      Juanina ;
   Lying, lying, lying,
In a slumber far more deep,
Than the stars of any night
Ever saw you sleep before,
      Juanina !

Nay, you will not ride again,
      Juanina !
Quietly, he, at your side,
Waits for some low word to chide ;
Waits for your soft hands' caress
To dispel the loneliness !
Waits, with patience stood apart,
Till some vague, unsolaced pain,
Some deep instinct breaks his heart,
      Juanina !

c

A WOODLAND WALK.

IT was Midsummer-time; a golden day
Whereon it seemed the floodgates of the sun
Were opened wide for every nook of earth
To feel Heav'n's wide beneficence of warmth:
The flowers, like unflinching baby-eyes,
Gazed upward through the breathless interspace;
The birds, scarce piping, drowsed upon the bough,
And dallying slipped the streamlet on its way.
And through the wood I walked with Juditha,
And as we went, in low and thoughtful tones,
She sang to me a little song I loved.

It is the merry mead-month,
    When rustic roses bloom;
And oh! the heart o' sycamores
    Is full o' scented gloom;
And rarely hang the golden lobes
    Upon the fragrant broom!

It is the merry mead-month,
    The grass falls 'neath the blade,

And oh! the heart o' every bird
   Sleeps silent in the shade,
And lightly rings the careless laugh
   From hay-time man and maid!

It is the merry mead-month;
   Would, would that it might be
As sweet a month to every one
   As 'tis to you and me!
God comfort all unhappy hearts
   Since this thing cannot be!

Then silence fell, and down the leafy aisle,
Like spirit-choristers, soft winds went by;
And from the censer-cup of nature rose
Many a subtle fragrance; and content
With silence wandered we, till once again
She, with sweet pathos, lingered o'er a song;

'Twas yesternight, 'twas yesternight,
   A year agone, my mother died;
There was not one to care for me,
   Not one less apt to love than chide;
Oh! long I wept; long, long I wept,
   Where I could chance unnoticed creep;
For may not e'en a beggar-maid
     Both love and weep?

'Twas yesternight, 'twas yesternight,
   A year agone, I crouched and wept;
But ere an hour had worn away,
   O God! how happily I slept;
No lady e'er could sweetlier rest
   'Mid down, and lace, and silken gleam;
No lady in the land e'er dreamt
     A sweeter dream!

I saw my mother stand by me
   In trailing robes of shining white,
With wings of dazzling loveliness
   That filled the dreary dark with light;
Her face had grown so beautiful,
   It drew the slow tears from mine eyes,
The longing tears to be with her
     Above the skies!

She laid her hand upon my hand,
   She drew my head against her breast,
" Ah! now, my child, my child," she said,
   " Content thyself with perfect rest!
Thou art no more, no more alone;
   Thou may'st not hear, thou may'st not see,
But I am evermore with thee,
     My child, with thee!

And that thou should'st remember this,
   And ease sad life' with memory,

From out thy place in Paradise
    Behold! what Christ hath sent to thee!"
She kissed me on my chilly lips,
    Her white wings faded o'er the land;
I woke, and found a holy flow'r
    Within my hand!

And as she ceased, lo! from a neighbour bough
A blackbird whistled shrill, and stopped, as 'twere
Ashamed too rudely to awake the calm,
So, once again, with a subdued delight,
Began its low and sweet soliloquy,
And chaunted on, with softness to the end,
Then preened each glossy wing, and flying left
The quiet more apparent to our hearts.   .
And I, "Oh! rarest of God's woodland bards!
How many centuries of troubled souls
Have eased themselves by list'ning to such strains!
Who knows but that, in far-off, classic days,
The dauntless blackbird piped its rustic lay
Sweetly as Pan his reeds Arcadian?
That many an one—thence by grim Charon rowed,
Disconsolate, unto the myrtle groves—
Less freely wept, for noting its rare song;
Poor Phyllis, 'plaining tardy Demophon;
Or she, around whose loved one's grave the elms
For ever grew, for ever died again
What time their climbing boughs caught sight of Troy!

Demeter might less sadly walk her meads ;
And Orpheus sing unto his lyre again,
Remembering submissively the Dead !
But I will e'en repay your minstrelsy.

Eurydice ! Eurydice !
If thou from Hades hearest me,
O plead with pale Persephone !
Breathe unto her of mead and rill,
The fragrance of the daffodil
Crushed 'neath her feet, when she was still
        A little maid in Sicily !

Implore her by my love, my longing,
The passionate thoughts perpetual thronging'!
Implore her by each sacred god,
Each Muse that steps Parnassus-sod !
Implore her by Hell's awful river,
The thunders of the Supreme Giver !
Implore her by sweet memory—
Yea, the sweet sake of memory—
That thou may'st come again to me,
        Eurydice ! Eurydice !

Could I have loved thee better, Sweet ?
    Nay, from the bright length of each hair,
Unto the fairness of thy feet,
        Thou wast to me beyond compare !

Day after day what I to thee
Thou wast a thousand-fold to me!
Night after night, when at thy side
  Beneath the happy stars I slept,
Oh! beautiful, my bride, my bride!
  My heart, undrowsing, ever kept
Its watch of utmost love o'er thee,
    Eurydice! Eurydice!

Thou can'st not hear, thou can'st not hear,
  Or thou would'st cast Death's wan disguise,
And pierce the fearful silences
  To answer my imploring cries!
    Eurydice, Eurydice!
  I break my heart for love of thee,
    Eurydice! Eurydice!

Then she—"It is too sad! too deep with pain;
No blackbird there has wiled away his grief!"
And I—"Content you! This next song shall be
Of yon soft southern clime, where thrushes fly
With busy zeal to help the vintagers!"

Not here, my fellow-Romans! Look not here!
  Stretch to some other eager foot and arm!
Back! back! Touch not the shadow of her hair,
  Or rose-flushed hollow of her tender palm!
    For Thalassius! For Thalassius!

What are these lips that you should long to touch?
  No redder than your own; and ah! what woe
Writ in their tender curves. Grieve not! wait; see
  How future days this present pain forego!
    For Thalassius! For Thalassius!

Crowd not; make room! The fire dies from her face;
  Her eyes, like stars o'er-blinded by the rain,
Are hid. Poor little lids weighed down with tears,
  Grief comes, grief goes, thou'lt lift and smile again!
    For Thalassius! For Thalassius!

Grieve not! thy kith, thy kin is here! To-day
  Fair Sabines mate with us! Hush thy regret,
Anon thou'lt love, in that the woman's heart
  All other pain and parting can forget!
    For Thalassius! For Thalassius!

Not here! not here! Romans, nought here for you!
  She weeps!—weep not, to-day thou art a bride,
And beautiful, and soon to be beloved!
  Thalassius for thee; thy chance is wide!
    For Thalassius! For Thalassius!

Then she—"I like and like it not! No sound
Of southern clime, of happy birds is there;
No sight of vines about that baby-Rome!
Nay, I can give a sweeter song than you."

From the land of Memory
    Wandering she went,
All the stars made melody
    In God's firmament.

Through a mist of tender light
    Vale and woodland shone,
Smiling went she, at the sight,
    As she looked thereon.

From the land of Memory
    Called he on her name,
Weeping soft and silently,
    Hasting back, she came.

"And yet again, if you will choose to hear."

It was the very heart o' days,
    When woodbines stilly bud and bloom,
And golden primroses of eve,
    With beauty fill the starless gloom;
We walked across the daisied mead,
    Just you and I, just you and I,
And overhead, far overhead,
    A woodlark singing 'gainst the sky.

The streamlet, babbling on its way,
    Now rose to sound, to silence died;

We crossed the little bridge, and still
   Went loit'ring, loit'ring by its side;
Just you and I, just you and I,
   And down upon the daisied lea
The happy lark that, lighting, spent
   Its last, sweet sob of melody!

Ah! love, how careless were we twain!
   We only felt the Summer-day
Enfold us with an influence
   More sweet than any words can say;
With wayward interchange of thought,
   How careless went we happy twain!
Thank God! divining not the time
   When we should meet no more again!

"Now you will wearied be! Canary-liké,
Made eager by surrounding circumstance,
I seem to sing against the very winds,
Careless of all save free delight of joy!
But daylight wears to dusk; anon the heart,
Like Egypt's god of silence—to the lip
The warning finger of profoundest thought—
Shall voiceless muse, contented with the calm.
Anon the eve shall shed her influence,
Grateful as dew unto the thirsty flow'rs,
And we in ever deeper quiet pass,

Divining the white Angel Presences
That closer watch the helpless hours of dark !
Now can you beat those little songs of mine ?"
And I, " Nay, you shall say !" and sang again—

My heart's to me a garden,
    Oh ! so rare ; oh ! so sweet ;
My soul at the gate stands warden
    'Gainst the tread of careless feet.

My thoughts for her are flowers,
    Her love is the life of each,
Her tears the tender showers,
    The sunshine, her smiles and speech.

She paces 'mid the roses,
    The pansies and mignonette ;
Where the heliotrope uncloses
    Its fragrant violet.

A tall white lily reaches,
    Grown beautiful and apart ;
Oh ! listen, love, what it teaches
    As it leans against thy heart !

Oh ! listen, my belovèd,
    Its words are these thoughts of mine ;
Oh ! listen, my belovèd,
    Till my thoughts are thoughts of thine.

Lean low! lean low! oh! warden!
Bid the careless feet begone;
The love that dwells in my garden
Is the love of two made one!

And when I ceased, no other words were said,
But Home we loitered, silent loitered we,
And when I looked upon her face, and saw
Its downcast tenderness of solemn thought,
Behold! I knew she gazed along the months,
And felt the end, so sad, so beautiful,
Wherein her heart for ever should resign
Its sacred dearnesses of liberty.
And the sun fell, and in the shining arch
Clouds, crocus-coloured as the festive-gowns
Of Attic maids at their Brauronia,
Motionless faded; homeward flew the rooks,
And the pale moon her dewy fingers laid
Upon the tirèd eyelids of the day.

TELEMACHUS.

ARGUMENT.

An Asiatic monk and martyr caused the gladiatorial combats at Rome
to be banished. In the year 404 A.D., in the midst of the amphitheatre
spectacles, he rushed into the arena and tried to separate the
gladiators. The spectators in the first moment of exasperation
stoned him to death. He was proclaimed a martyr by the Emperor
· Honorius, who soon abolished the combats.

HE cares not for you! Hurl your hardest; do your
    worst;
Curse with more unction now than ever you have
    cursed;
Account it noble, tender women, to have thrown,
With ready zeal of rage, the merest dole of stone,
And glory to have struck him! 'Tis nigh done! Did'st
    heed
How, swifter than the Thracian prince's snow-white
    steed,
And straighter than the arrow to its mark, he sped?
And 'tween the wrestling creatures pressed hands, feet,
    and head,
Imploring arms, and cries that tried the heart-strings, so
Brimful were they of almost more than human woe!

He might have been a god, immortal, free from death,
So fearlessly he faced it! With hard-bated breath
One minute there we sat. Mute, as a stricken bird,
Each watcher forward leant; no silken garment stirred
Above the fragrant heaving of a woman's breast;
The dallying hands were still; impatient feet at rest;
Soft glances frozen to a horrible, wide stare,
Smiles hardened to a grin, laughs on the vacant air
Died, mocking at themselves! Life hung suspended o'er
That unit in the wide arena, then, once more
Relaxing, spent its gathered strength in such a cry
As tears the throat of Hell! Thou foolish monk! to try
And balk the wild beasts of their lawful prey! See how
The flame of hate burns white on wrathful lips, eyes,
  brow;
Hear the shrill tumult clamour nearer round his life!
He cares not! Still upon the gladiator's strife
Presses unfaltering; flings his poor, puny strength,
Straining against the knotted arms, and corded length
Of hard, withstanding limb. What is his hand to them?
The passing touch of some frail woman's garment hem
Would move them more! He speaks! hot words of
  holy grace
That die unheard amid the thunder of the place.
Great drops of sweat roll down his anxious brow,
  worn, meek,
And sad. What is't? A stone! it marked him on
  the cheek,

And now again, again! See how they part and fly
Who strove before him! Thick as hail through
    thunder-sky
The whistling missiles speed. See the bent form.
And still these hungry Romans scream and rage and
    swarm,
Like carrion birds about a putrid feast! He sinks,
O horrid sight! O horrid sound! Thud, thud, that
    drinks
One's strength away. He sinks, he falls!
                         Amid the crowd,
The Emperor lifts his hand, signs quiet, speaks, and
    loud
All lips applaud his words, "The monk just dead,
    acquaint
The world, we do requite with reverence as a saint!"

A BALLAD OF LOVE AND DEATH.

WHO is it at the outer door
   With finger-touch so slight?
She passes through or passes o'er,
   I cannot see aright;
She passes up the darkened house,
   Herself her only light.

For she is clothed in shining white
   That lightens up the stair,
Clothed whitely from her chilly neck
   Unto her feet so bare,
Which shine as cold as the river-drops
   That hang about her hair.

There is no echo of her step,
   No creak beneath her tread;
She goes where all is strange to her,
   As though a lover led,
And her face is grey and pallid as
   The face of one just dead.

She pauses at the chamber door,
　　She passes through to find;
Each footstep o'er the rugless floor
　　Leaves a wet print behind;
She shakes with silent sobs as though
　　She shook beneath a wind.

He holds deep dreams beneath his lids,
　　He does not hear or wake;
Far off, he dreams, she waits for him,
　　Where happier mornings break;
Far off he speeds, they meet and sit
　　Where silver aspens shake.

She lays her chilly face to his,
　　He clasps her in his sleep;
Across his eyes that dream and smile
　　Her tears and sighings creep;
He clasps her close and starts awake
　　To hear her weep, and weep.

" Nay, sweet," he cries, cheek close to cheek,
　　" Nay, sweet, and what is this?"
" I could not die," she moans to him,
　　" Without a parting kiss;
My spirit cannot leave the world
　　Without your parting prayer;
D

My spirit cannot pass," she moans,
    " Tho' my body's lying there !"

He's kissed her on her weeping eyes,
    He's kissed her on her lips,
He's kissed her on her shining hair
    'Whence the chill water drips,
And softly between every kiss
    A word of praying slips.

" The river was more dark," she moans,
    " Than your dark eyes, my love ;
And whiter even than your face
    The moon was white above ;
More swiftly than your kisses, love,
    My feet slid through the grass,
The water drowned my breath away,
    But my spirit could not pass.

The wild winds tore, the great tree shook,
    I clung against its branch,
The great tree cracked, it met the wave
    Like a cruel avalanche ;
The waters clasped me like your arms,
    They bubbled at my lips,
They chilled me cold, they chilled me dead,
    Unto my finger-tips ;
Feel, love, how cold and dead I am,
    See how the water drips.

I could not smile and live, my love,
  Since first I heard them tell,
That we should be as far apart
  As Heav'n's height is from Hell;
But I could not die in quiet, love,
  Without your kiss and prayer;
My spirit strove to you for that,
  Though my body's lying there.
Now swifter than my feet that slid
  So swiftly through the grass,
From your warm arms and kiss and prayer
  I feel my spirit pass."

His empty arms fall to his breast,
  His kiss comes back no more;
One pallid ray of moonlight falls
  Across the silent floor;
He sees the footprints, dark and wet,
  Lead to the fastened door.

They lead him down the gloomy stair,
  And o'er the threshold space;
Adown the fields, amid the grass
  They leave a shining trace;
They lead him where the great tree lies
  Across the river-place,
She rocks amid the floating leaves
  With a smile on her drownèd face!

PERSEPHONE'S SONGS.

FROM SICILY.

I.

"Through the dewy morn I go."

THROUGH the dewy morn I go
  With my maidens fair and sweet,
Blue above, and golden glow
  Of daffodillies at our feet.
While the birds with folded wing
  Dream a sleepy melody,
And the syrens softly sing
  On the shore of Sicily!

Thou art fair as Time is old,
  Thou art fragrant by the rills,
And my gown is touched with gold
  From thy kisses, daffodils!
While the birds, with waking wing,
  'Gin a tender melody,

And the syrens sweetly sing
  On the shore of Sicily!

As thou lov'st me, come away,
  I will leave no flow'r forlorn,
Some of thee I'll take to-day,
  Some of thee to-morrow morn!
Oh! the birds, with troubled wing,
  Pipe a mournful melody;
And the syrens sadly sing
  On the shore of Sicily!

II.

"When a lover comes to me."

When a lover comes to me,
  In Sicily, in Sicily!
We will walk beside the sea
To hear the syren's melody;
  We will fragrant Hybla climb
  To watch the bees amid the thyme;
With daffodillies in one hand
We will loiter o'er the land,
    In Sicily, in Sicily!

Daffodils might fill each hand
  In Sicily, in Sicily,

But that, ah! I understand
　　A far sweeter maiden's whim,
　　The other shall be held by him,
As we loiter o'er the land
　　In Sicily, in Sicily!

FROM HADES.

I.

"I dreamt of a lover."

I dreamt of a lover,
　　Oh! spare me, oh! spare me!
Away from my mother,
　　Dark king, would you bear me?
Kiss me not, love me not, clasp not my hand,
Desolate, desolate, lieth the land!

Though with you for ever,
　　I am not your bride!
Though leant close together,
　　Oh! the distance is wide!
Let me forth, let me forth, like a bird o'er the lea,
My mother is seeking and weeping for me!

II.

" Behold ! amid the Shadows dim !

Behold ! amid the Shadows dim,
 I sit beside their dark-browed king ;
I weep, yet never think of him,
 For over earth awakes the Spring ;
And oh ! with breaking heart I know
The daffodils of Enna blow !

Would, would I were a maiden now,
 As in those far-off, golden days,
The vivid sunshine on my brow,
 My footprints left 'mid dewy ways,
Where, oh ! with breaking heart I know
The daffodils of Enna grow !

" I know not, know not, what I would."

I know not, know not, what I would,
 So sad, so desolate am I ;
A mournful soul of alien ways
 I droop beneath the shining sky,
What time the Spring-days beckon me
Back to my mother's Sicily.

No more birds' songs I joy to hear,
　　No flowers can I love again,
The vivid light mocks at my woe,
　　The sunshine pierces me with pain;
Behold ! I am too sad a thing
For Nature's happy summering !

Better amid these Shades to sit,
　　These colourless and scentless flow'rs;
Better amid unsmiling brows
　　To wear away the weary hours !
I have forgotten how to be
A happy maid of Sicily !

A HUNTING BALLAD.

"It's oh! my bonny mare, my bonny, bonny mare,
The wind from the South knows the quiver of thy mouth,
And the clouds o'er the sky know the brightness of
    thine eye,
  As thy heart beats wild and hotly for a-hunting;
And it's neither here nor there if my soul be dull
  · with care,
For the ugly, black dog flies when I look into thine eyes,
  And know we two together go a-hunting.

"It's oh! my bonny mare, my bonny, bonny mare,
We'll be off and away through the soft morn dull
    and grey,
Through the grassy summer lanes, turning brown with
    autumn rains,
  To the common where the gorse was once a-yellow;
And there they all will come, some chatting and
    some mum,
With the spurs a-clank, a-clink, and the young bucks
    dressed in pink,

And the time-worn hands in garments aged and mellow;
And there we two shall wait with our hot hearts both
    elate,
And for all that I can say, 'tmay be right for thee to
    pray
    The " find" may be some tough, long-winded fellow!

" It's oh! my bonny mare, my bonny, bonny mare,
I could kiss thee 'tween thine eyes, where the velvet
    white star lies,
For the human tenderness of thy gentle look's caress,
    Ere thou and I together go a-hunting;
And my heart in time shall beat to the music of thy feet,
When the hunter's moon 'gins burn at the hour of our
    return,
    Together, both together, from a-hunting!"

He sang it blithe and gay, that early Autumn day,
As strong and dark he rode on the gallant mare that
    strode
    To the cover where the gorse was once a-yellow;
And off, off, and away! at the foxhound's mellow bay,
No one as he that day rode half so straight away
    At the heels of that old, tough, long-winded fellow!

The low wind of the South blew on the mare's soft
    mouth,
The glimmer of the sky lit in her flashing eye

As her heart it beat in rhythm with her rider;
But she did it at the last when the village street was
    pássed;
She did it at the bank where the boldest 'mid them
    shrank
    To see her stagger up from a crushed form stretched
    beside her!

No more, no more he'll ride, at the early morning-tide,
    When the dew is still on grass and flower lying;
No more, no more he'll turn, when the early stars
    'gin burn,
    And the even-winds of Autumn soft are sighing;
No more, no more he'll hear the hunter's horn sound
    clear,
    And woods and hills reiterate the calling;
No more, no more he'll wist his bonny mare can list
    The words of love that from his lips were falling:
But well I know if now the warmth came to his brow,
    And he could have one wish for death's beguiling,
He'd kiss her 'tween her eyes, where the velvet white
    star lies,
. And fall asleep contented, calm and smiling!

IN ARCADIA.

I.

PAN PIPING.

PAN piping in Arcadia,
  His syrinx to his lips,
And on it, lightly up and down,
  His dancing finger-tips!
Oh! trip it, trip it, trip it,
  Come oreads, light and fair,
  Come naiads, and trip it there,
  With the rushes 'mid your hair,
    In sweet Arcadia.

Though dewy dusk steps down the hill,
  And drowsy flocks go by,
We'll dance no more before the sun,
  But 'neath a starry sky.
So trip it, trip it, trip it,
  Come satyrs, dance your fill,
  Come gay nymphs, trip it still,
  For Pan is piping with a will
    In sweet Arcadia!

What matters flight of foolish time,
  Hushed birds and closing flow'rs;
What matters aught but happiness
  To fill the careless hours!
Oh! trip it, trip it, trip it,
  Come dryads, leave the tree,
  Come happy fauns, and happier be,
  For Pan is piping merrily
    In sweet Arcadia!

II.

PAN AND ECHO.

He leant, and piped an idle tune,
  Unwitting that she listened,
And oh! he played so tenderly,
  Tears on her eyelids glistened,
And one, beyond her own command,
Fell down upon the player's hand.

He turned, and lo! another strain
  That all gay things resembled,
And oh! he piped so cunningly,
  Smiles on her young lips trembled,
And one, too eager in its part,
Fell down upon the player's heart.

MOORLAND MEMORIES.

AMID the purple ling we lie;
A lark's flight nearer to the sky
Than they who, in the busy street,
With brows thought-weighted, pass and meet;
Such thought as here hath not its part,
So much a knowledge fills the heart
Of God's prevailing love and care,
Of angel-wings that throng the air,
And the upholding of that Hand
By which our highest good is planned.
Above us, happy hour by hour,
Light .as the rowan's feathery flow'r,
Or downy plume on birdling's breast,
The clouds, full-sail, scud from the West;
The shadows fly, now heath, now grass
Feel their cool wing-prints as they pass,
O'er crag, o'er dell, o'er babbling stream
They glide as voiceless as a dream,
Then climb the hill and dip from sight
Toward the realms of earliest night.

Brown as elm-seed in latter May
The poising hawk hangs o'er his prey;
The curlews, glancing low and high,
Give forth their soft, pathetic cry;
The swallows, vocal flecks of joy,
Forget the Autumn-time's alloy
Of weary flights o'er trackless seas,
And fierce, 'mid-ocean melodies;
The grouse brag loud; and, oh! Love, hark
The passion of yon mounting lark,
That, with its rare, wild minstrelsy
Sings there,—so would I sing to thee—
As though unto some chosen star,
Or that, through Heav'n's gate slipped ajar,
It deemed the Angels might be stirred
To love to listen to a bird.
How beautiful all nature now!
With wide content of upturned brow,
And listening looks of radiance,
She seems, like patriot Joan of France,
To hear, o'er her deep breaths of prayer,
Heav'n's whispers tremble through the air.
The valley, nestling at our feet,
Where tenderest of colours meet,
Opes wide and warm, serene and calm
As that, thereafter, piercèd palm
When to each child-like, faithful one
It gave its loving benison.

Below the purpling heather-rim
The brackens, straightly tall and slim,
Under their wide-crowned greenness keep
Soft quietudes of shade and sleep:
Thence, lower still, come flowery spots
Of hare-bells and forget-me-nots,
Brown-blooming reeds, beloved of Pan,
'Mid runlets, scarce a foot in span;
White orchis, poising soft and light
As butterflies prepared for flight;
Shy daisy-maids in pink-tipped frills,
And that dark rose that loves the hills,
What time more rarely may be heard
The hum of bee and song of bird.
Yet, further down the cool incline,
'Tis but a step to reach the kine,
The farmstead and the rustic bridge,
The ferns on either stream-bank's ridge,
The silver gleams of leaping trout,
And gnats that madly whirl about,
Like they who, 'neath the linden tree,
Went through their rustic revelry,
When, sinless, up the neighbour-street
Passed beautiful-faced Marguerite.
So soon, profoundly hushed and dumb,
The stilly even-tide hath come;
No voice disturbs, from hill or sod,
This tender peace, so born of God!

The sun is set; now into night
Deepens each almond blossom light;
The cloudlets, flushed as maple-shoots,
Or purple as the vineyard fruits,
Now gloom, now pale, now steal away
Like boats from out some sunny bay;
The stars grow clear; and ah! watch how
Above yon sombre mountain-brow—
That, solemn-faced as Memnon, sees
The onward roll of centuries—
The moon comes up; now like the rim
Of some rare, gold-lipped goblet brim,
Held out in hail companionship
By gods toward the mortal lip;
And now like some—as more and more
Ascendant from the Eastern shore—
Terra-celestial loveliness,
Too full of Heav'n's height to express,
And yet of earth so vocal-clear
That, melting through the human-ear,
It with its golden fingers starts
The vesper-music of our hearts.
So upward, its deep, tidal grace
Thrilling the starry interspace,
With motion most melodious
It leans its steadfast looks on us,
Even as they that Dante sings
Who, with extended Angel-wings,
E

All night upon the dark heights kept
Watch o'er each travelling soul that slept
In Purgatory's circled pale
Of slumber-silent, misty vale.
Come down, come down! Thy name I lip,
And dream of thy companionship,
Though thou art far 'mid rich and poor,
And I alone upon the moor,
Where many a golden memory
Associates itself with thee.
'Twas here the happy hours I wiled,
I lay and thought of thee, and smiled;
Here, hill and dale before me spread,
Thy written words I read, re-read,
And every time of reading o'er
Still found them sweeter than before;
And there, I, months past our farewell,
For many an hour, through many a Hell
Of conflict, struggled to attain
A Heav'n of calm content again!
Ah! should we, tow'rd the end of days,
Meet somewhere on our alien ways,
How would it be? Would'st thou, o'er all
Life since has borne, those days recall?
Or wonder still to see arise
The deathless passion in mine eyes?

THE LYRE.

SEVEN were the strings of the lyre
  First fashioned, that filled
  The heart of the god with the thrilled
And tempestuous desire.

Seven times over his fingers
  Sprang clear from the strings,
  And his soul was away on the wings
Of earth's untroubled singers.

Seven times still the vibration
  With softness recurred,
  And his life to its centre was stirred
By the trembling pulsation.

Then Apollo, the gracious and tender,
  "Give this unto me,
  And the gold rod of wealth unto thee,
With my heart's love, I'll render."

And Hermes, the crafty and cunning,
  "The thing is for thee,
  If unto my Pan's-pipe and me
The flocks shall come running!"

So, wandering off o'er the meadow
  And pasturage sod,
  Soft-stepped, went Apollo, the god,
Through sun and through shadow.

With caressing of tremulous fingers,
  Lit unto the strings; ·
  And his soul was away on the wings
Of earth's untroubled singers.

Seven were the strings of the lyre;
  And they, 'neath his hand,
  Breathed the spirit of ocean and strand,
Of rainfall and fire.

The secrets of earth—primal mother
  Of human and god—
  And wild things that haunt sand and sod,
Innate foes to each other.

The painless forth-bringing of flowers,
  The song-life of birds,
  The breathing of slumbering herds
Through eve's dew-footed hours.

The sighing of sad, homeless zephyrs,
　　The patter of rains,
　　And over the pastoral plains
The lowing of heifers.

They told of the fair, divine daughters,
　　Virgin Athené,
　　Heré, and white Aphrodite
Born from foam of the waters.

They told of all life, love, and longing,
　. A human may know;
　　Of speech, tender-trembling and low,
With contented thought thronging.

Yea, of fancies too lovely to capture,
　　Far off as the spheres,
　　Till mortal and god wept hot tears
Of ineffable rapture.

MAIDEN SONGS.

IONE.

THERE came a maiden over the sea,
Who laid her touch upon my hand
As she walked along o'er the golden sand,
    And looked at me;
    Ione, Ione.

The light of the shimmering, summer sea
Shone in her beautiful eyes;
I thought I was looking on Paradise
    For eternity;
    Ione, Ione.

We walked by the tremulous summer sea;
All earth, all heav'n I then forgot,
Past and present remembered not,
    Nor things to be;
    Ione, Ione.

A white-winged boat came over the sea;
She hid her eyes, she loosed my hand,
And stepped on board off the golden sand,
    And sailed from me;
    Ione, Ione.

Across the waste of the moaning sea,
Some one will wed her by-and-by,
But that any could love her more than I
    Can never be,
    Ione, Ione!

ELIZABETH.

She held a flower in her hand;
  A mist of tears o'er-brimmed her eyes;
  She answered me, half words, half sighs,—
Both tender as a summer land,—

"This bud is all I have for thee,
  To seal our long companionships."
  She put the flower to her lips,
And reached it through the gloom to me.

I took it, trembling, in my hand,
  Her eyes with mine communing met,
  "And yet," they breathed, "I love you yet;
I love you! Can you understand?"

Oh ! God, there is a higher good
   Than self's unquestioning happiness,
   Though reached unto with hard distress,
And bitter to be understood !

DELIA.

   Dear little Delia !
With her laughter and her chatter,
Her sweet, shy smiles and glances,
And her wayward April-fancies !
A rosebud maid was Delia,
A bud that never would unclose,
   Or let the petals slip apart
Into the perfect open rose ;
A rose-bud that was tip-kissed up
Above the pink corolla-cup
   Of her little, wayward heart.

   Dear little Delia !
We never cared to win a peep
   Within the silence of your heart ;
We thought it still was fast asleep
   To life's distress of grief and smart !
   How could we, could we doubt
   But that, because so fair without,
   The rose was also fair within ?

Yet all the while you learnt to bear,
With child-like smiles, your woman's share
  In mournful heritage of sin.
And down, deep down, all night, all day,
The slow tears fell, the heart was sore,
The hidden dole of anguish wore
  Your heart away.

    Dear little Delia!
Who would have thought you could have died?
  Or lived, except as young and gay,
  Until the wide world passed away?
Who would have thought you could have slept
  A sleep so undisturbed as death,
  Without those sweetest smiles to chase
  Each other o'er your tender face,
  And laughter bubbling in your breath;
Without your mavis-mellow voice
Persuading others to rejoice;
Without your gay lips moved to chatter,
  And your soft, bare, little feet,
With a rhythmical, light patter
  Stirring o'er your chamber floor?
Oh! memory, too sad, too sweet,
  Never, never more
  In this long life to be
  Aught but a memory;
    Dear little Delia!

LOVE'S PETITION.

I ASK no sound of thy remembered voice,
　　No last look at thy face,
No knowledge of thy ways along the world,
　　No place against thy place;
I ask to do no service in thy cause;
　　Though if, beside thy feet,
I but might labour, toil, and strive for thee,
　　Oh! God, how sweet, how sweet!

But this I ask not; nor to ever take
　　The first, the foremost place
In any secret sweetness of thy thought,
　　The tumult of thy heart;
Content were I, beloved, content indeed
　　To fill the lowest place,
To know thou could'st divine a presence there
　　No changes might efface.

Forget me as thou wilt; forget my all,
    My love, my life, the while
Some happy one, some best-beloved of thine
    Receives thy look, thy smile;
But if through loss my love thou should'st recall
    To comfort thee in pain,
Than this no more I ask, except that thou
    May'st soon forget again.

LOVE'S SERVICE.

WOULD that I might have laid these hands in thine;
These hands, weak as a human hand may be,
But strong with courage that were all divine
    If taxed for thee!

Would that I might have laid these hands in thine,
Faithfully warm through life's cold destiny,
For ever o'er all shadow and all shine
    To work with thee!

Would that I might have laid these hands in thine,
Through the long, mournful days there have to be—
When this and that of joy thou must resign—
    To comfort thee!

But since this is not, and God knoweth best
To whom our service in this world must be,
These hands content themselves, together pressed
    In prayer for thee!

SPRING SONGS.

I.

MARCH WINDS.

OH! for the March wind, and the March sun,
        And the March rain,
That go wild together upon the hill!
Oh! for the trees that never are still,
And the mad, inconstant rains that fill
Young flower-cups and honey-combed vein
Of primrose leaves, till wild winds spill
        Them out once more!
The glorious wild wind from the Western shore.

He comes from the Western shore,
His wings are wet with the spray
From the billows, crested white,
        And the hollows grey;
His voice has brought the roar
Of the ocean's tempestuous calling,
And it sounds across the land
Like the sweep of a wave upon the sand,
        Rising and falling.

Oh! for the March wind, and the mad wind,
      And the wild wind,
That sweeps through the hanging wood;
Oh! for the flush, and rapture, and rush,
      And stir in the blood,
As the wind cometh over the moorland,
      And over the lowland,
That lies like a misty, unbreaking billow
      Down in the hollow
'Tween hill-side and hill-side!

Oh! for the feeling of wild exultation;
      Like a lark, winged wide,
Mounting and singing, and singing and mounting,
With the wind beating, pursuing, and meeting;
      Glorious, tumultuous.
Oh! for the March wind, its rage and its roar!
The fetterless wind from the wild Western shore!

II.

A LARK'S SONG IN MAY.

Oh! love, love, love,
I must away, I must away!
Nay, love, entreat me not to stay,
    Entreat, entreat me not.

Some passion of supreme delight
Bears me from pastures, dew-bedight,
O'er stream, o'er quiet mountain-height
Half veiled in mists of morning light!
   Entreat, entreat me not!
'Tis thine to brood so low and still,
I must against the sky fulfil
   The mission of my lot.

Fear not that any flight of cloud
Thee from my furthest ken could shroud;
   Nay, at Heav'n's very gate,
I look from countless heights of space
Upon thy love-illumined place;
The careless flowers' nodding grace
About thy nest I seem to trace,
    And thee, and thee,
    Sweet love, I see,
Sit patient, waiting for thy mate.

Oh! cloud on cloud, I mount me higher!
Oh! flushed trees, trembling into leaf!
Oh! youth of joy, oh! last of grief!
Oh! tenderness of Spring's desire!
Now every bird hath built his bower,
Where April fringes with its shower
The sweets of leaf and bud and flower!

Now every bird hath won his mate
With wooing hot and passionate;
And high and low, and wide and far,
'Neath flooded light and single star,
From glade, and height, and woodland, starts
The music of contented hearts!

Oh! love, love, love,
I come again, I come again,
With wings that touched the cloudlet's rain!
I come again, I come again,
With rapture that is almost pain!
Oh! love, love, love,
I come to thee,
I come to thee.

III.

IN MAY.

Now Spring toward the distance dim
Steps soft and loth across the land;
She gathers up the flowers she sowed
And bears them, drooping, in her hand;
The Proserpine-loved daffodil,
The primrose scattered on the lea,
The fragrant-hearted violet,
And fragile-faced anemone.

The faded blooms from windy March,
  The tear-wet buds from April's rain,
Each love-gift that earth loves no more,
  She takes unto herself again;
Then, lifting up her life-flushed arm,
  On which the timid birdlings rest,
She wafts them back to Home once more,
  And fades adown the golden West.

A fairer one shall take her place,
  With butterflies, like prismèd loves,
Courting the clustering May she brings,
  And roses, white as Venus' doves;
Touching with soft, caressing wings
  The odorous buds in sun-warmed spots,
The delicate, uncurling fern,
  And tender-eyed forget-me-nots.

Ah! gracious days, as bright and.fair,
  And growing thick with vivid green,
As when the Royal lover leant
  From out his open lattice-screen,
And, unaware, looked down and saw
  One in the sweet May garden space,
Unconscious, happy as a flower,
  With early summer on her face.

F

Ah! gracious days, as lovely now
    As when those two thus learnt to love;
Ah! happy hours, whose sunny lights
    Too quickly unto even move;
'Tis life to see a flower live,
    To feel the rapture of the lark,
And list the mated thrushes drop
    Their vespers down the gentle dark!

HUNTING SONG.

"Hark, for'ard, away!" Through the morn soft and grey
    The words come and go;
And my good mare and I tremble through at the cry
    Of the bold Tally-ho!

Off, off with the first at the life-stirring "burst,"
    We followed away;
Our breaths deep and steady, our hearts bold and ready,
    For a hot run that day.

For the scent was breast-high, and to do or to die
    The one thought of my soul;
A red dog-fox led, the hounds streamed ahead,
    And we raced to the goal!

Half wild with delight at the pigeon-like flight,
    O'er the open we flew;
And my gallant, tried mare, with the best of them there
    Galloped steady and true.

Full-cry, off around the steep hill-side they wound,
        Through the fence, o'er the ditch;
"Who follows," men said, "in a trice will be dead,
        Or be devil or witch!"

I sat still and steady, my heart light and ready
        As a feather that's blown;
She flew o'er like a bird, not a single twig stirred,
        And we went on alone!

Oh! maddest of rapture, for a creature to capture
        Scarce once in his day;
And good-bye to dull care when I and my mare
        Hear "Hark, for'ard, away!"

MNEMOSYNE.

She paused, compelled by memory to stay
   The feet too eager for the lagging heart,
   That, flooded o'er with thought,—like Fate apart,
Sad-eyed, divining all,—took Life's survey.
Round her enfolding dusk, and through the grey,
   Against the fragrant heart of roses leant,
   Sad Philomel across the silence sent
Sweet melody, and sang eve's heart away.
From out her hand, unconscious of its loss,
   Some fading flowers, softly, one by one,
Fell at her feet upon the dewy moss.
   Too deep for tears, the grief of days far gone
Gazed from her eyes, as, down Time's shadowed track
She, o'er her shoulder looking, yearned far back !

A LEGEND OF FAITH.

SHE slept. And at night's midmost gloom
An Angel lighted in the room;
" Come," low he breathed and tenderly,
    " Some hearts ere nearing God o'er-brim
With earthly suffering." And she,
    In spirit, rose and followed him.

Along the quiet streets they went,
O'er meads and pastures dew-besprent;
Through sleeping woods where larches hung
    Their feathery tufts of tender green,
And many a Spring wild flower flung
    Sweet odours to the blue serene.

'Mid hill and dale they patient trod,
O'er thorny path and daisied sod;
Past haunts where woodland songsters small
    In sleep forgot their vespers sweet;
He led her tenderly through all,
    Unto a far-off city street.

"Come," still he breathed, "thyself prepare
For this worst woe thou hast to bear;
Rememb'ring, whatsoe'er there be
  Of griefs thou canst not understand,
This truth should all avail for thee,
  God's deeds to noble ends are planned!"

A latch he touched, and from the gloom
Led her within a shining room,
  Where whispered speech, and shout and song,
  And curses loud, and deep, and long,
And clink of glass and laughter high,
  With careless words of mockery,
  And sounds of horrid revelry,
Burst upward to the solemn sky.

There, many a one-time guileless face
Had long abjured its maiden grace;
There, kiss and oath together ran
  As at a Devil's feast of feasts;
And God's divinest image, man,
  Was lower than the very beasts.

And lo! upon her stricken glance,
Flashed a belovèd countenance;
  Unlovely with unlovely thought,
  With passion's vilenesses distraught;

And from his lips a murmur fell
That would have raptured inmost Hell!

Then she, her tortured gaze turned low,
With long, sick shudderings of woe,
Unto the listening Angel spoke,
   "Behold, I love him; love him much!"
And into sudden sorrow broke,
   'Neath the compassion of his touch.

"I asked no thing from God of love,
No charm of deed, of look to move
His alien heart unto my heart;
   I only asked in ministry
To him, to take my humble part;
   Content, whate'er the toil might be!

"Oh! hours of tears; oh! days of prayer;
Oh! months and years of aching care;
Oh! anguish of requited hope,
   Too bitter to be understood;
Is all in vain with God to cope,
   In pleading his eternal good?"

The. Angel then, "Ask God still less,
To satisfy thy happiness!"
And she, "Nothing I ask! I trust, oh! God;
   Some day, some way the battle won!

My fevered haste by faith o'er-trod;
  Thy will, Thy own best way be done!"

And with her eyes' sweet radiance
Scanned the belovèd countenance;
  Nor shrank, nor paled with anguish fear,
  As once again upon her ear,
From 'tween his lips, the murmur fell
That would have raptured inmost Hell!

Then turned, but on her trembling hand
The Angel laid his hand's command,
  "That thou should'st pass, it was not meant,
  Unto thy earthly tenement;
Return, return again with me,
And see the human left of thee!"

The latch he lifted, and once more
Led her without the sinful door;
  O'er meads and pastures dew-besprent,
  O'er hill and dale they silent went,
Until at morning's tender gloom,
Lighted within her quiet room.

And lo! one lay, and on her face
Tear after tear had left its trace;
  Tear after bitter tear, the while
  Her lips were parted with a smile.

The Angel then, " Read thou the token ;
At the first word by thy love spoken,
Behold! thy human heart was broken !
  Come now with me, and learn aright,
  Reward of Faith, how infinite!"

BY THE SEA-HO!

THE stars are bright,
The moon's alight,
The fish-boats rock from left to right,
  For the eastern wind is high-ho ;
    It rushes o'er
    The ocean shore ;
The billows rise with a crash and a roar,
  As though to touch the sky-ho !

    On a narrow ledge
    Of the grey cliff edge,
Where callow guillemots might fledge,
  A girl leans crouching down-ho ;
    She looks across
    The waves that toss,
And thinks of the grief, and sorrow, and loss
  To fall that night on the town-ho !

Far out, away
Beyond the bay,
A fisher-boat rides wild and gay
    Upon the seething foam-ho ;
        Now low, now high,
        And the sea-gulls cry,
And the girl looks out 'neath the shining sky
    To the boat that will ne'er come home-ho !

In the highest tree
Beside the sea
Three crows sit dark as dark can be,
    Staring across the waves-ho ;
        They sit and think,
        While their dull eyes blink,
Of the billows that roar at the grey cliff brink,
    And the myriad ocean graves-ho !

The wild clouds ride,
The cold stars hide,
The night's wings stretch forth far and wide,
    And the crashing billows ebb-ho !
        Below the cliff,
        Like a sea-beat skiff,
A fisher-lad lies cold and stiff,
    Wound in a sea-weed web-ho !

So still he lies
At morning-rise,
A girl leans smiling to his eyes,
And treasures his death-cold hand-ho !
While swinging by,
With a mocking cry,
Three crows across the sea-shore fly
Heavily o'er the land-ho !

A VISION.

AMID the purple heather of the moor—
That rises, Titan-like, from out yon vale
Threading the golden West—lying, through deeps
And deeps of solitary thought I sank,
When on my startled ear a sigh arose
Beyond all earthly sounds of utmost woe,
And far adown the shining slopes I saw
A vision that can never pass from mind.
Behold! around the mountain's shoulder came,
In silent order, mournful forms of gloom,
Dark-robed, dark-stol'd, with folded pinions,
Blacker than nights forsaken by the stars ;
And still, with noiseless footsteps, still they came,
And, passing, ever took their onward way
Beside the windings of the moorland stream.
And lo! to lead the path, an Angel went,
Of dazzling loveliness that shamed the sun ;

White-robed was he, and on his shining brow
The perfect peace of knowledge that perceived
Christ conquer o'er the furthest woe of Time!
Yet, as they passed, once more arose that sigh,
As from a world of breaking hearts that poured
Their anguish in one voiceless breath to God!
Some, through sad tears, gazed forth upon the fields,
The piping birds of happy Summer-time;
Some, with imploring eyes, looked unto Heav'n,
Or earthward bent their faces' hopelessness;
Whilst o'er the patient lips of happier ones
The trembling promise of a coming smile
Broke, beautiful with largest faith in Love!
Then, at my side, a shining Presence spake—
" Lo! these are they who died far fallen short
Of Death's immediate fulnesses of joy;
Who through the cycles of God's punishment
Strive for the sinless Courts of Paradise!
These suffer still! Remembrance and Remorse,
The Fire, the Worm of Hell, torture each heart!
No sound, no sight, but doth again recall
A very anguish of sad memory;
No memory but acheth o'er the woe
Of good that was not, but which might have been!
And unto them the Angels minister;
With influence of word, of deed, of love,
Assisting the endeavour of each thought
Toward the rising of the perfect day

When on the low-bent brow of Penitence
Forgiveness lays the healing of its hand!"
Then silence fell, and round the mournful crowd
Innumerable Angels hov'ring sang,
Until across the suffering eyes of grief
There flashed a glory of supremest Faith!

LOVE'S AFTERMATH.

ONE time, my heart, rose-like amid its leaves,
  Contented dwelt, nor dreamt of larger things,
  Till Love, the sun,—with warm and od'rous wings,
And eyes, clear as the harvest-moon that weaves
Her tender light 'mongst early russet sheaves,—
  From o'er it charmed, delicate fold by fold,
  Soft petallings, and to the dewy cold,
And farewell swallow-songs from rain-fringed eaves
It op'ning, looked upon the face of Love!
And lo! night came! and, roaring far above
  The flaming woodlands, hollow winds went by,
  With scudding sounds of dreadful mockery,
And slow storm-drops, whose scorching lightnings fell
Like happy memories on those in Hell!

G

A WOMAN'S WISH.

If thou would'st draw me to that heart of thine,
　Make me companion of thy truest self.
　Bring forth no gold, none other than the delf
Of daily life, to serve the food, the wine
Of thy thoughts' present minist'ring to mine;
　Scatter no needless flowers o'er the path
　Lest we should reap their scentless aftermath
'Mid days despoiled of our faith's summer-shine.
Let me stand equal in thy joy and grief,
　With smiles requiting that, with comfort this,
　Howso it be but some low word of bliss
Divinely taught to me for thy relief;
Yea, let me feel, whate'er of fortune comes,
My heart for evermore thy Home of Homes.

LOVE'S REMEMBRANCES.

I DO not ask God that I may forget
  The very least of thy remembered ways,
  The far-off shining of those golden days
When it was granted that we sometimes met:
Thy looks, thy smiles I sit and think of yet;
  The thoughtless tricks of gesture and of speech,
  It doth content me to remember each,
Howso with anguish of heart-sick regret:
And still,—although so oft within my heart
I feel the tears of keenest sorrow start,—
  I could not, best-beloved one, ever pray
  A single sweet of memory away;
I only ask, when I such joys recall,
With resignation to remember all.

INFLUENCE.

Ah! strange! year after year slips by—
As gently as adown eve's tender hush
The tender vespers of some happy thrush
Wakeful for love's sake 'neath the star-lit sky—

Short years of striving to the goal,
Of labour equalised by labour's love:
Long years of loss, of alien thoughts that prove
Unchanging severance 'tween soul and soul.

Thy name, these days, I scarcely hear,
I can keep count of glances at thy face;
While unto thee unknown my voice, my place,
Far-off these footsteps that were once so near.

Passed from each life! Still this not all!
Some other hand may comfort thy dear hand,
Some stronger soul in thy heart's vision stand
To walk with thee where once my way might fall.

Ah! strange! yet love some other one,
So that it be for thy best happiness;
O'er all, through all, thou art to me no less
Than in the days of our communion!

As then, so now, and to the end;
Remembrances of thee evangels are,
Thy past approval still the guiding star
To deeds that thou might'st even more commend.

Whate'er I win, take thou some praise!
The influence of that far-off joy of ours—
Like treasured gifts of scented woodland flow'rs—
Shall shed sweet fragrance to the last of days!

YESTERDAY.

'Twas yesterday the world was young,
    Birds' voices filled the sunny noon,
And flowers their faint perfumes flung
    Along the pathways of the moon.
But yesterday hath no returning,
O vain regret, O fruitless yearning!

'Twas yesterday our loved ones lived,
    And walked by us amid the flow'rs,
With gentle deeds, communing words,
    And looks that answered love to ours.
But yesterday hath no returning,
O vain regret, O fruitless yearning!

'Twas yesterday the heart felt glad,
    A smile, a word could give delight,
And every thought its radiance had,
    Like stars that glorify the night.
But yesterday hath no returning,
O vain regret, O fruitless yearning!

'Twas yesterday! Oh! foolish plaint,
  Could hearts endure a twice-told way,
Already they beat low and faint
  With struggling once through day by day.
But yesterday hath no returning,
O blessedness of fruitless yearning!

AN EVENING SONG.

In thicket and dell sang the nightingales,
  So low and long, so soft and sweet ;
  And the delicate coolness of grass to our feet
Felt fresh as the meads of Thessalian vales,
  Where, touching his lyre by sheepfold and pen,
  Apollo made happy the children of men ;
And oh ! in a passion of tenderest pain
The Summer night wept and was quiet again.

Light shook the leaves 'neath the soft, southern wind,
  And the stars were out and the moon was high,
  And the phantom cloud-ships sailed through the sky,
And left the beautiful world behind,
  As white, and as wan, and as tender as she
  Who was spared of the children of Niobe ;
And oh ! in a passion of tenderest pain
The Summer night wept and was quiet again.

Oh ! beauty of Heav'n, of woodland and lea,
   Oh ! time of contentment too peaceful, too pure,
   Behold ! in contentment I could not endure,
And thought, inarticulate, rushed over me,
Till my heart, in a passion of tenderest pain,
Like the Summer night, wept, and was quiet again.

LOVE'S MELODIES.

OH ! tuneful hands of Love, I pray thee play
   Thy truant melodies on my heart's strings ;
   No matter of what changeful fashionings,
If now a Psalm, and now a roundelay,
A sobbing grief, a thought part sad, part gay,
   That, lark-like through the morning's glory, springs
   With ever climbing and impatient wings ;
No matter how thou playest if I may
   But feel thy delicate, slight fingers thrill
   The memories long grown so mute, so still,
And hear across the land the Summer leaves
Whisper soft orisons 'neath starry eaves,
   Till Happiness smiles upward to the sky,
   And Sorrow, hearkening, goes downcast by.

SUFFICIENCIES.

IF I had known it were so deep a pain
   To fill life's sweetest intervals with song ;
   To pass, companionless, the busy throng
Where careless lives go smiling, twain and twain ;
For ever, far beyond all loss, to gain,
   And ever, far beyond all gain, to long
   Toward possession still more full, more strong?
If I had known how little and how vain
   The deepest anguish of dumb thought to reach
   The consolation of a perfect speech?
If I had known? Oh! God, I question not
The wide beneficences of my lot,
   Than this indeed I ask no higher thing,
   Still let me suffer, and still let me sing.

Marcus Ward & Co., Printers, Royal Ulster Works, Belfast.

www.ingramcontent.com/pod-product-compliance
Lightning Source LLC
Chambersburg PA
CBHW032204010726
47493CB00008BA/2821